Magic Ballerina

Delphie and the Magic Spell

Welcome to the world of Enchantia!

I have always loved to dance. The captivating music and wonderful stories of ballet are so inspiring. So come with me and let's follow Delphie on her magical adventures in Enchantia, where the stories of dance will take you on a very special journey.

p.s Turn to the back to learn a special dance step from me...

D1189117

Special thanks to
Linda Chapman and
Katie May

First published in Great Britain by HarperCollins *Children's Books* 2008
HarperCollins *Children's Books* is a division of HarperCollins *Publishers* Ltd,
77-85 Fulham Palace Road, Hammersmith, London W6 8JB

The HarperCollins *Children's Books* website address is
www.harpercollinschildrensbooks.co.uk

1

Text copyright © HarperCollins *Children's Books* 2008
Illustrations by Katie May
Illustrations copyright © HarperCollins *Children's Books* 2008

ISBN 978 0 00 785909 2

Printed and bound in England by
Clays Ltd, St Ives plc

Magic Ballerina™

Delphie and the Magic Spell

Darcey Bussell

HarperCollins *Children's Books*

*To Phoebe and Zoe, as they are the inspiration
behind Magic Ballerina.*

Contents

Prologue

In the soft, pale light, the girl stood with her head bent and her hands held lightly in front of her.
There was a moment's silence and then the first notes of the music began.
For as long as the girl could remember music had seemed to tell her of another world – a magical, exciting world – that lay far, far away.
She always felt if she could just close her eyes and lose herself, then she would get there.
Maybe this time. As the music swirled inside her, she swept her arms above her head, rose on to her toes and began to dance…

The Bluebird's Dance

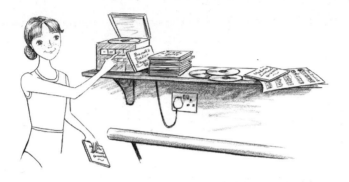

The ballet studio was quiet and still. It could only be a couple of hours since it had been full of girls dancing for their ballet teacher, Madame Za-Za. Now there was just one girl left.

Delphie Durand pressed the button on the CD player and then ran lightly to the centre of the room. She waited for the music to start, one foot slightly in front of the other, her head bent, her eyes looking down at her red ballet shoes. All the other girls in her class had pink ones but it wasn't just the colour that made Delphie's shoes different from theirs. Delphie's ballet shoes were also magic!

Madame Za-Za, the owner of the ballet school, had given them to Delphie three weeks ago. She'd told her they were very special but Delphie hadn't known just how special until two nights later when the shoes had started glowing and sparkling. When Delphie had put them on, they had whisked her away to Enchantia – a magical land where all the characters from the different ballets lived. A land full of incredible adventures!

Delphie smiled as she remembered the adventure she'd had there. It had been scary but amazing! Just then, the first few notes of the music swelled out from the CD player. Delphie quickly pushed thoughts of Enchantia to the back of her mind. She had to get this dance right.

She heard the music she had been waiting for and glided forward into a run, taking tiny steps as she skimmed across the floor. As the music changed, she stopped on her tiptoes, looking from side to side like a bird, her arms held

13

slightly behind her like wings. *Wait*,
Delphie told herself, listening to the music
carefully. *One, two...*

She danced forward and turned a
pirouette, before travelling forward again
and stopping with one leg held behind
her, one arm in front,
trying to look as if she
was a bird
flying. All of
Madame Za-Za's
instructions from the
class earlier ran through
her head – lift the chin...
shoulders down... keep
your back strong... turn
out that leg...

14

Delphie was so busy thinking about the placing of her leg that she lost her balance and stumbled. Bother! It was so hard trying to concentrate on everything at the same time. Before she had started ballet classes, she had simply danced just how she had felt. Now she was learning that you had to make sure every bit of your body was doing the right thing at the right time. But Delphie found that when she concentrated on her legs, she forgot about her arms and then she remembered them and realised her head was wrong and her shoulders were up and by the time she had got those right, her legs were wrong again.

But I've got to get it right, she thought as she walked back over to the CD player to restart the music. *There's only one day to go!*

The very next morning there were going to be auditions for the school's end of term show. It was a woodland ballet and the main part was the Bluebird. All of Delphie's class wanted to be the Bluebird. Delphie had been practising and practising.

The door to the studio opened and Delphie saw Madame Za-Za look in. A slim, elegant woman with her greying hair pulled back into a low bun, she was wearing a long floaty skirt over footless tights and a wrapover top.

"Well, Delphie?" she said. "How is it going?"

As Delphie met her teacher's gaze, she couldn't stop the truth from bursting out. "Actually, I'm not doing very well, Madame Za-Za. I just can't seem to get the

dance right no
matter how hard
I try!"

"Maybe you are
trying *too* hard,
child," Madame
Za-Za said.

Delphie frowned.
"What do you
mean?"

"It will make sense one day, Delphie,"
Madame Za-Za said with a smile. "Maybe
sooner than you imagine." And with that
she left the room.

Delphie sighed, restarted the music
and went back to the centre to try again.
But even the very first run felt wrong and

stiff as she tried to think about her feet,
arms and head all at once. She broke off
with a groan and went to stop the music
before glancing at the clock on the wall. It
was nearly time to go. Her mum and dad
would be home from work.

With a sigh, Delphie went over to the
wooden barre that ran around the edge of
the room and began to do some slow
stretching exercises. She was just finishing
when the door opened.

Delphie looked round, expecting to see
Madame Za-Za again, but in her place
stood Sukie Taylor. Delphie's heart sank.
She was in Delphie's ballet class and was
very, very good at ballet, but she didn't
seem to like Delphie at all.

Sukie looked surprised to see her. "Oh. Hi. I left something." She picked up a pink cardigan from the back of a chair and switched off the music. "What are you doing here?"

Delphie shrugged. "Just practising."

"For the auditions?" Sukie's eyes narrowed. "Well, you won't have a chance.

You've only been coming to classes for three weeks and Madame Za-Za has pretty much said that I'm going to be the Bluebird. Everyone knows I'm the best dancer in the class."

Delphie swallowed. *Just ignore her*, she told herself. She didn't want to get into an argument.

"You never know," Sukie went on. "Maybe if you try hard enough you'll get to be a rabbit or something."

Delphie watched as Sukie smirked and flounced out, then Delphie pulled a face. Sukie might think she didn't have a chance but no one would know until the actual auditions. *I might be the Bluebird*, Delphie thought hopefully. She crossed her fingers. Oh, she *so* hoped she would be. But first she just needed to get the dance right...

A Noise in the Night

"Mum, come and see this bit!" Delphie
called after supper. She was sitting on the
sofa, her feet curled under her, watching
the ballet of *Cinderella*. She had been given
the DVD for her birthday. It was her
favourite scene where the fairy godmother
changed the pumpkin and mice into a
coach and horses and then transformed

Cinderella from a servant girl in rags into a beautiful princess.

Mrs Durand came through to the lounge and sat down beside Delphie on the sofa. "Maybe one day you'll be able to dance like that," she said, stroking Delphie's long brown hair. "Wouldn't that be wonderful?"

Delphie snuggled up to her mum. "Oh yes," she breathed. There was nothing she wanted more in the world.

At bedtime, Delphie kissed her mum and dad goodnight and went upstairs. As she got into her nightdress, she looked hopefully at her red ballet shoes sitting on her desk. *Please sparkle tonight*, she willed them. *Please!*

But they looked as still as ever, just as they had every other night that week.

Every evening she had lain in bed, willing
the shoes to glow, hoping to hear music in
the air, just like she had the first time they
had taken her to Enchantia.

It would be just so amazing to go back,
Delphie thought as she got into bed, after
brushing her teeth
and hair. *I'd love
to see Sugar the
Sugar Plum
Fairy again, and
all the other people I
met, like the Nutcracker
and the waltzing flowers and the dancing
snowflakes.* She shivered as the image of a
rat's face with red eyes, long whiskers and
sharp teeth popped into her brain. The one

23

person she wouldn't want to see again was the evil King Rat! He hated dancing and was always trying to stop it. Delphie had been to his castle and met him and his mouse guards and it had been very scary!

To try and stop thinking about it, Delphie focused on the audition the next day. She began to go through the steps of the dance in her mind, practising them over and over again, and before she knew it she was drifting off to sleep…

Delphie's eyes blinked open. She felt sure that something had woken her. Sitting up, she glanced at her bedside clock. It was just past midnight.

Suddenly she heard a faint noise. *Music!*
As she listened it grew louder. Delphie
looked at her desk. Her red ballet shoes
were glittering and shining like rubies.
Throwing back her duvet, she jumped
out of bed and ran over to them. Did this
mean another adventure was about to
begin?

Delphie picked them up, her fingers
trembling in excitement. The first time she
had gone to Enchantia
the shoes had
whisked her off
to a theatre. Delphie
tied the ribbons
of the shoes in
anticipation.

As she tied the bows, her feet started
to tingle. She stood up and the feeling
whooshed all the way from her toes up to
her head. A second later, she was swirling
around in a myriad of colours – pink,
purple, blue, red, yellow, orange, green...

And then she landed with a bump to find
herself sitting on a red seat, in the same
darkened theatre that she had arrived at
before, only this time the air was very cold.
She shivered and rubbed the bare skin on
her arms. The stage was shut away behind
red velvet curtains. Music started playing
and the red curtains began to open.

Delphie jumped up eagerly and then
caught her breath. It was all so different. The
first time she had been here there had been

light and colour, the scenery had shown mountains, fields and a village, as well as King Rat's castle and there had been lots of characters on the stage even though they had all been asleep. But now the background scenery was just painted white and the stage was empty. The floor was covered in a thick blanket of snow. There were bare trees on the stage, their branches covered in icicles.

Delphie walked hesitantly down towards the stage. "Sugar?" Her voice echoed through the empty auditorium. She didn't like this. There was a feeling in the air as if something was horribly wrong.

"Sugar!" she called uneasily. "Where are you?"

The Glittering Palace

Just at that moment, a flash of blue zipped across the stage. Delphie's brown eyes widened as she saw a beautiful turquoise bird about the size of a robin. It landed on one of the icy branches and sang loudly, its tiny wings fluttering, its head cocked on one side.

"Hello," Delphie said, going up the steps at the side of the stage and looking at the little bird. "Do you know what's going on?"

"Yes!" the bird twittered.

Delphie was only a little bit surprised to find that it could talk. She was in Enchantia after all!

"My name's Skye," the bluebird said. "Are you Delphie?" Delphie nodded and the bird carried on. "I've been waiting for you. Sugar thought the ballet shoes might bring you here again. We're in terrible trouble, Delphie."

"Trouble? Why?" Delphie asked in alarm.

"King Rat has cast a spell over Enchantia to make it winter all the time," Skye told her. "He has a model of Enchantia sealed inside a glass globe. Whenever he shakes the globe, snow swirls around and then it falls in real life too.

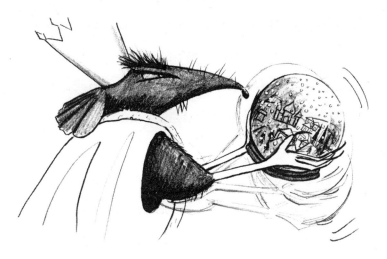

When it's as snowy and icy-cold as this no one can dance properly."

Delphie shivered as Skye continued.

"Everyone just stays indoors and all the animals and birds have either hibernated or gone away to where it is warmer. All my family have flown off. I hurt my wing though and couldn't keep up with them so I had to come back." She dipped her head and looked very sad. "I really miss them. I wish it was spring again so they would return. But King Rat says he'll only break the enchantment if he can marry the King and Queen's daughter, Princess Aurelia, and she doesn't want to marry him at all."

"I'm not surprised!" said Delphie.

"But if Aurelia doesn't marry him it's going to stay winter forever," Skye sighed. "Sugar is at the palace now, trying to comfort the princess. Do you think you might be able to help us? I can show you the way there."

"I'll try!" promised Delphie. "Let's go!"

"It's this way!" sang Skye. "Follow me!"

The bluebird flew off the stage and Delphie ran after her, finding herself in a

wood. There were tall dark trees rising up
on either side and the air was totally still
and silent apart from the sound of Skye
singing as she swooped on ahead.

Delphie ran as fast as she could.
It helped keep her warm.
Luckily her ballet shoes
didn't seem to
get wet.

"Here we are!" the bluebird called finally as she flew out of the woods.

Delphie stopped with a gasp as she looked up at the palace in front of them. It was made of glittering white marble and had tall pointed turrets, a moat that had turned to sparkling ice and a big golden door.

"It'll be warm inside," Skye said, tapping on the entrance with her beak.

The door opened and a large, cheerful-looking guard looked out.

"We're here to see Sugar," Skye told him. "I've brought Delphie, the girl with the magic ballet shoes."

The guard beamed. "Everyone's been hoping you'd arrive," he said to Delphie. "My name's Griff. Come in! You must be freezing out there."

"Thanks!" Delphie hurried into the castle. Through the door was a high-ceilinged hall with richly embroidered tapestries. There were three huge log fires burning and the warm air wrapped around Delphie like a hug.

"Here," Griff said, coming over with a purple velvet cloak. "Put this on until you've warmed up."

The material was soft and thick and
Delphie pulled it snugly around her.

"I'll go and fetch the King and Queen,"
Griff said. "We're in awful trouble. I really
hope you can help us this time."

Delphie shivered. She hoped so too.

Delphie's Plan

Griff hurried off. A few minutes later, he returned with four other people – a beautiful girl with long brown hair wearing a pink dress and a delicate silver tiara, a woman in a midnight-blue dress, a man wearing dark trousers, a gold crown and a purple fur-lined cloak and…

"Sugar!" Delphie exclaimed in delight

as she saw her friend the fairy. Sugar
looked just as she had the first time Delphie
had seen her and was wearing a pale lilac
tutu, tights and ballet shoes.

Sugar grabbed Delphie's hands and
swirled her around. "It's great to see you
again, Delphie!" They stopped and hugged
and then the smile faded from Sugar's face.
"Has Skye told you what has happened?"

Delphie nodded. "King Rat is totally evil!"

"He certainly is," said the princess,
coming forward. "I'm Princess Aurelia, and
this is my father and mother, King Tristan
and Queen Isabella of Enchantia."

"Welcome to our palace, Delphie," King
Tristan said. "It's a pleasure to meet you."

Delphie wasn't sure what to do. She had

never met a king and queen before. She swept her leg behind her and curtseyed gracefully, keeping her back straight, just like she had to do at the start and end of every ballet class. She saw Sugar's look of approval and glowed.

Queen Isabella came forward and took her hands in hers. "I really hope you *can* help us.

"Yes," said Princess Aurelia desperately. "I don't want to marry King Rat but if it's the only way of stopping Enchantia being frozen in winter forever, then I will do it."

"Surely there must be something else we can do," said Delphie. "Can't someone just steal the globe or something?"

"We've tried," answered Sugar. "But it's impossible. King Rat won't let it out of his sight. He says that the only thing that will make him break the globe is if he marries Aurelia – today!"

"I'm going to *have* to marry him!" Princess Aurelia's eyes filled with tears. Her mother and father quickly comforted her.

Delphie's thoughts tumbled over each other. What could they do? There had to be some other way…

Suddenly there was a very loud croaking sound from just outside the window. Delphie jumped. "What's that?" she said, covering her ears as the noise came again even louder.

"Oh, that's Priscilla the toad," said Sugar. "She's been croaking like that ever since the moat froze over," said Princess Aurelia. "It's *really* annoying."

There was another loud croak. Delphie looked out of the window. An extremely large, extremely grumpy-looking toad about the size of a large dog, was sitting on the ice of the moat.

"She croaks all day and all night unless she's eating," said the King. "It's impossible to sleep! I wish she'd go away."

"We'll do something about her soon, dear," said the Queen soothingly. "Maybe Sugar can use her magic to turn her into a nightingale or a mouse or something for a while – anything that doesn't make such a dreadful noise. But first we have to decide what we are going to do about King Rat."

The Queen's words gave Delphie an idea.

"Maybe we can do something about *both* things at the same time!" she said.

"What do you mean?" asked Princess Aurelia.

A grin spread over Delphie's face. "Sugar, could  you really use your magic to turn Priscilla the toad into something else?"

"Yes," replied Sugar, looking confused. "But what would I turn her into?"

"If you turned her into a beautiful princess – the most beautiful in the whole of Enchantia, even more beautiful than Aurelia, then I bet King Rat would want to marry her instead," said Delphie.

"Of course!" gasped Sugar but then she frowned. "But how would that solve our problem about it being winter? King Rat wouldn't have to break the enchantment if he wasn't marrying Aurelia."

Delphie had thought about that. "All we have to do is say that the new princess will only marry him if she can have a sunny day for her wedding."

"It's a brilliant idea," said the Queen. "Although Sugar's magic only lasts a few hours – things can only be transformed for the length of a ballet, no longer."

"We'd have to be quick then," said Delphie. "And get King Rat to marry Priscilla straight away."

"That shouldn't be too hard. Everything

will be in place for the wedding," said
Aurelia. "He was going to marry *me* today.
All we need is for him to decide to marry
Priscilla instead."

"We'll have to be careful though," said
the King. "If King Rat sees Sugar and me
and the Queen and Aurelia, he's bound to
know that there's some sort of trick going
on. He's very clever."

"Well, you could all stay here and I'll go with Priscilla. I could pretend to be her assistant." Said Delphie. "You don't think King Rat would recognise me from the time I helped the Nutcracker escape, do you?"

"Oh no, King Rat may be clever, but his memory is terrible!" Sugar replied. "I think it's a wonderful idea, Delphie."

"And I could fly on ahead and spread the news that a mysterious princess is coming," chirruped Skye. "A princess who *everyone* wants to marry."

"It might really work!" said Sugar in delight.

Delphie grinned at everyone. She loved the thought of tricking King Rat. "Then let's do it!" she cried.

A Toad in Disguise

It wasn't long before Priscilla was fetched in from the moat. She sat in the hall, looking crossly at them all, her dark eyes glaring out from her brown and green bobbly, wrinkly skin.

"This is going to take quite a lot of magic," Sugar said with a sigh.

Delphie giggled. It was very funny to

think of King Rat marrying Priscilla. They'd explained to the toad what was going to happen and all she had done was croak grumpily.

Sugar pulled a wand out of her tutu, stretched her right leg forward and then rose on to her pointes, closing her left foot neatly. Music magically swelled out into the room as Sugar swept forward. She pirouetted round Priscilla and then jumped into the air, one arm held to the side, the other above her head as she flew into the air. She landed lightly and danced on.

Delphie's feet tingled. As she watched Sugar dance, she almost felt as if she was doing the steps herself, as if *she* was the one

spinning and leaping, keeping every movement light and delicate, her head poised, her arms outstretched.

The music rose in volume. Sugar stopped with one leg lifted and bent behind her, her right hand pointing her wand at Priscilla.

There was a flash and a
cloud of lilac smoke.
As the smoke
cleared, the music
stopped and Delphie
gasped. Priscilla was
still in front of them
but she wasn't a toad
anymore. She was a
beautiful brown-haired
princess with enormous
dark eyes. She was wearing a
moss green and yellow dress, which
sparkled with jewels. A heavily embroidered
cloak hung from her shoulders and she was
wearing a tiara with a gold veil that trailed
behind her to the ground.

"Oh wow," Delphie breathed.

The King, Queen and Princess all clapped.

The toad princess's tongue shot out and she caught a fly.

Sugar giggled and came down off her pointes and dropped into a graceful curtsey. "I am pleased to present Princess Priscilla from the mysterious land of Toadonia," she said, with a grin. "And now all the princess needs is a horse-drawn sleigh!"

A little while later, Delphie sat on the front seat of a beautiful silver sleigh that was being pulled by two white horses that Sugar had conjured up from a pumpkin and two white mice just like in *Cinderella*.

51

The horses had green and gold plumes on
their harnesses and gold bells hung from
the leather reins. Griff was driving.
Priscilla sat behind Delphie, a white fur rug
across her knees. She looked so beautiful, it
was almost impossible to believe she was
the toad until she opened her mouth and a
croak came out.

Even Sugar's magic couldn't make her speak!

"I think I'll have to put a spell on her so she stays silent," said Sugar, shaking her head as Priscilla croaked again. Sugar turned a pirouette and pointed her wand. Priscilla opened her mouth but no sound came out. The toad princess looked very surprised.

"Here, Priscilla," Sugar said. She magicked a bag of dried flies and handed them to the toad. "You can have these to make up for not being able to speak." Sugar looked at Delphie. "You'd better get going."

"OK! See you later!" Delphie said, pulling the warm rugs around her.

And so the sleigh set off. As the horses cantered away, their hooves sent up clouds of sparkling snow and their breath looked like steam in the frosty air. The wind rushed through Delphie's hair and she laughed in delight as Griff urged the horses on and the countryside raced by.

About twenty minutes later, a dark castle loomed up in the distance. "King Rat's castle," Delphie breathed, remembering it from before. She wondered if Skye had got there and passed around the news about the princess. She didn't have long to wait to find out.

Six of King Rat's mouse guards were standing on the roadside, dressed in leather waistcoats with swords hanging from their belts. They were each as tall as Delphie. One of them stepped out into the road and held up his paw, bringing the sleigh to a halt. "Who are you?" he called. "Declare your names!"

55

Delphie's heart beat faster as she stood up in the sleigh. Would they believe her? What if they realised it was all a trick? Their swords looked very sharp. She took a deep breath and hoped her voice wouldn't shake. "This is Princess Priscilla of Toadonia!" she declared. "And I am her Royal Assistant."

One of the guards, a tall skinny brown mouse, pushed his way past the guard at the front. "King Rat has heard about the Princess. Is it true she's the most beautiful princess in the whole of Enchantia?"

So Skye *had* been there spreading the word!

"It's absolutely true," Delphie declared. She swept Priscilla's veil back. The guards' eyes widened. Priscilla really did look beautiful.

"The princess is looking for a husband," Delphie told the guards. "There are many lords and princes who want to marry her. But she has heard about King Rat and she believes that he might be her perfect match. Take us to him!" she instructed grandly.

To her delight, the guards swung round. "Follow us!" said the lead guard and dropping down on to all four feet, the guards scampered off down the road.

Delphie heard King Rat before she saw him, coming from one of the open first floor windows.

"Where is this Princess?" he was shouting in his harsh voice. "I want to see her. She can't be more beautiful than Aurelia. She…" He stopped as if someone had just spoken to him. "What?" he said sharply. "She's here?"

King Rat suddenly appeared at the window. Delphie gulped. He looked just as frightening as she remembered him.

His nose was pointed, his whiskers were long and sharp, and his beady eyes gleamed red. He was wearing a spiky gold crown and a long gold cloak and was staring at Delphie. "Well, *she's* not very beautiful," he began, pointing at her. "She's just a child and rather a small one at that…"

"I'm not the princess!" Delphie stepped to one side to display the newly transformed princess. King Rat looked at Priscilla. For a moment he didn't say anything and then a smile crossed his face. "Now, she *is* beautiful!"

Priscilla opened her mouth but no sound came out.

"What's she saying? What's she saying?" demanded King Rat. He preened his whiskers.

"And what does she think of me?"

Delphie cleared her throat. "The Princess has a sore throat at the moment and can only whisper." She bent towards the toad princess and nodded as if Priscilla was talking to her. "King Rat, my princess says she has never seen such a fine figure as you, your majesty. She compliments you on your... your..." Delphie racked her brain. "On your wonderfully curling whiskers," she invented, "and your very shiny fur! She would just *love* to be your wife!"

King Rat smoothed his paw over his greasy fur. "Well, of course, people do say I am very handsome," he said haughtily. "And she is certainly more beautiful than that Princess Aurelia." He leaned out of the window. "Very well. I *will* marry you, Princess!" he called to Priscilla as if he was doing her a huge favour. "I will marry you – today!"

Delphie grinned at Griff. This was going well! "The Princess is very pleased," she told King Rat. "But she says she will only get married on a sunny day."

"But that means I would have to take my spell off Enchantia," King Rat frowned.

Delphie bent towards Priscilla and then looked at King Rat again. "The Princess will certainly not get married in the wintertime."

"Oh very well," King Rat said, looking at the princess. "Just for you, I will break the spell."

"Now?" said Delphie hopefully.

"Now!" declared King Rat. "Well, just as soon as I have got myself ready." He blew a kiss towards Priscilla. "I will be down in a few moments, my love," he said, pulling his lips back and revealing his pointed teeth in what he obviously thought was a charming smile.

As he disappeared into the castle, Delphie breathed a sigh of relief.

"It's worked!" said Griff in a low voice, and Skye twittered in delight.

Patiently they waited as King Rat stomped around, shouting at his servants. "Get me my biggest crown! No, not that one, you idiot! The one with the rubies in. I must look my very best for my bride!"

"I hope it doesn't take him *too* long to get ready," Delphie hissed to Skye and Griff.

The minutes ticked by. At long last there was a blast of trumpets. The great wooden door of the castle was thrown open and

King Rat came marching out. He stopped and threw his arms open, as if expecting a round of applause.

There was a moment's silence. King Rat started to frown and then his guards realised what he was waiting for and hastily began to clap.

Delphie only just stopped herself from giggling. The King's whiskers had been tightly curled, and he had put oil on his greasy fur so it was slicked back and gleaming. Looking very pleased with himself, he preened vainly. "Well?" he called, looking at Delphie. "What does my princess think?"

Delphie looked round at Priscilla, preparing to make something up. She froze. Priscilla's face was turning brown and green and wrinkly. King Rat had taken so long getting ready that Sugar's magic was wearing off. Priscilla was turning back into a toad!

In Trouble

Delphie felt as if a bucket of cold, icy water had just been tipped all over her. What was she going to do now? She leapt forward and hastily pulled the veil over Priscilla's face, feeling very relieved that King Rat was so busy posing that he wasn't looking too closely at his bride-to-be.

From under the veil came a croak.

"What's that awful noise?" asked King Rat.

"Just the princess coughing," said Delphie hastily. "Coughing and saying how much she… um… she loves your curling whiskers."

King Rat smirked. "Of course she does."

There was another croak – even louder this time.

"And she *really* loves your shiny fur," Delphie babbled, trying to drown the sound. "But she says she'll only marry you if you're wearing a crown with emeralds, not rubies."

King Rat looked thoughtful. "I suppose emeralds would bring out the colour of my teeth. Very well, wait inside the hall while I get my spare crown." And with that, he hurried back into the castle.

Griff drove the sleigh as close as he could to the castle door and then jumped down as he and Delphie helped Priscilla into the hall. She was getting shorter and squatter by the moment. In just a few minutes she would have turned completely into a toad!

"Oh no, what are we going to do?"
Delphie gasped as soon as Griff had shut
the door behind them. She looked
anxiously at the staircase where King Rat
had gone.

"If only Sugar were
here," said Skye. "She
could do the dance
again and turn Priscilla back.

Delphie looked thoughtfully at the
bluebird. "Does it *have* to be Sugar who
does the dance?"

The bluebird shook her head. "No, in
Enchantia, magic comes from the dance
itself."

"Then maybe I could do the dance?"
Delphie gasped.

Just then, King Rat's voice called down
the stairs. "I'll be down in a minute, my love!"

"There isn't a moment to lose!" said Griff.
"Quick, Delphie! Please try!"

"I won't be able to do it exactly," Delphie
said hurriedly. "Because I can't dance on my
pointes yet. But I can have a go!" She took a
deep breath. Could she remember what
Sugar had done? She thought she could. Her
feet started to tingle in the red ballet shoes.

Sweeping her arms up, she rose on to her
demi-pointes. She remembered what Sugar
had done and danced forward, her arms
stretched out, her head up, hearing the
music in her head. She moved into a
pirouette, danced forward again and then
leapt into the air just as Sugar had done.

She couldn't quite manage it but she jumped as high and gracefully as she could before landing lightly. Bringing her right leg round, she stepped on to her right foot and lifted her left leg high behind her, pointing her hand at Priscilla just as Sugar had done. Delphie held her breath. Would her dancing have been good enough?

There was a flash of light and Priscilla
changed back to a princess!

Skye gave a loud chirrup of excitement.
The dance had worked!

"Well done, Delphie!"
said Griff in delight.

Delphie ran forward
and threw back
Priscilla's veil. The toad
looked like a beautiful
girl again – and just in time
as King Rat came hurrying down the stairs.

"I am here, my love!" he called. He was
now wearing an ornate crown with
emeralds in. "Let us get married!"

"First it's got to be a sunny day," Delphie
reminded him.

72

King Rat pulled a glass globe out of his pocket and strode outside with Delphie, Griff and Skye following him eagerly. Inside the globe, just as Skye had said, there was a little model of Enchantia. A few snowflakes were drifting around the model just as they were outside.

King Rat put the globe down in front of him and clapped his hands. "Break!" he commanded sharply. There was a loud cracking noise and the glass shattered.

Immediately, the grey clouds parted and the sun shone through. The air grew warmer, the snow on the ground began to melt, the ice on the moat cracked and the bare branches of the trees burst into green leaf.

"It's spring!" Delphie cried, looking round as the snow melted quickly and bright blue, yellow and pink flowers pushed their way up through the grass.

"Hrumph! I suppose it is," said King Rat grumpily. "Still never mind that. I am going to get married now!"

"To a toad," Delphie whispered to Griff and Skye, with a giggle.

King Rat turned round and headed back towards Priscilla. "Come along, my love. We will be married straight away."

Delphie, Griff and Skye dashed away.
The sky was blue and the sun was shining.
Birds swooped through the air, twittering
and singing. Looking at the woods,
Delphie saw brown rabbits poking their
noses out of their burrows and squirrels
appearing from holes in tree trunks.

Suddenly there was a flash of light.
Delphie blinked as Sugar, Princess Aurelia,
King Tristan and Queen Isabella appeared
at the edge of the woods.

"Delphie!" the Princess gasped, running
forward. "You've done it! You've made
King Rat break his enchantment!"

"We saw winter change to spring and knew
your plan must have worked," said Sugar.
"So I used my magic to bring us here."

"We can't thank you enough!" said King Tristan.

Delphie glowed. She was so glad she had been able to help! "I had to do the dance that you did," she told Sugar eagerly. "The magic started to fade and Priscilla began to turn back into a toad."

"You must have danced it really well to make the magic happen," said Sugar. "But if you weren't dancing on your pointes, the magic might not last as long as last time."

"I wonder just how long it will last?" Delphie said anxiously.

Suddenly there was an ear-splitting yell from inside the castle. "What? My princess is a great big, green slimy TOAD!"

Springtime!

As they looked behind them, they saw
Priscilla come hopping out of the castle.
She charged among the guards, sending
them flying as she went this way and that,
croaking. Then suddenly she spotted the
muddy waters of the moat around King
Rat's castle. Looking very happy, she gave
a loud croak and dived in.

King Rat came charging out, shaking his fist at Delphie. "You tricked me! You... you..."

Priscilla surfaced and gave a croak so loud that everyone covered their ears.

"Go away!" King Rat shouted to the toad.

Priscilla looked at him smugly and croaked even more loudly.

"I think Priscilla likes it here!" grinned Sugar. "She looks like she's going to stay!"

King Rat looked like he was about to burst with rage. "Get me some ear plugs!" he yelled at his guards. "And lock these tricksters in the dungeons!"

The guards lunged towards them.

"Hold on, everyone!" shouted Sugar, turning a pirouette.

There was a bright flash. Delphie felt
herself spinning through the air. The next
moment she had landed back outside the
royal family's glittering marble palace
along with everyone else.

"We're back!" she cried in relief.

"And we're not the only ones!" exclaimed Sugar. "Look!" She pointed into the sky.

Delphie gasped. A flock of bluebirds was flying towards them.

"It's my family!" chirruped Skye, racing to meet them before disappearing joyfully into the group.

"Thank you, Delphie," Sugar said, taking Delphie's hands. "It's almost time for you to go back home but we'll see you again, I'm sure!"

Delphie didn't really want to go but before she had a chance to feel really sad about leaving, Sugar waved her wand.

"Let's all dance!"

Light, bright music filled the air. The Princess, the King, the Queen, Sugar and even Griff began to dance. The bluebirds swooped around them.

"Join in with us, Delphie!" Skye chirruped.

The music swept through Delphie. She danced forward, the bluebirds encircling her in a glowing cloud. Delphie copied their delicate movements, running in tiny steps on *demi-pointes*, feeling as light as a feather. She spun into a pirouette and then went forward again, stretching her arms out like wings as the bluebirds fluttered and sang about her. Delphie raised her arms above her head, reaching into the sky

towards the fluttering birds. She sprang upwards four times, crossing her feet over with every jump. The joy of dancing filled Delphie. She had never felt so light or so graceful. It was like she was a bluebird herself. Suddenly she seemed to spin faster and faster. Colours swirled round her and she was swept into the air…

The Big Audition

She landed to find herself standing in her
bedroom, her head still spinning from the
dance. She looked down at her ballet shoes.
They glittered for a moment and then
returned to their usual red colour.

Smiling, Delphie knelt down and undid
the ribbons. What an amazing adventure!
She put the ballet shoes on her desk and

wriggled her toes. She was tired and her
muscles ached but she felt very, very happy.

Quietly, she got into bed. As she shut her
eyes she pictured herself dancing with the
bluebirds. She hadn't worried about her
arms and her legs, she'd just listened to the
music and danced. Was that what Madame
Za-Za had meant earlier when she said it
was important not to try too hard?

Delphie snuggled down. She couldn't
wait until the audition the next day!

The music swelled out in the ballet studio.
Delphie danced forward, lost in the
sound. Madame Za-Za was watching but
Delphie was hardly aware of her teacher.

She reached up above her head and then sprang lightly upwards, landing softly through her knees each time. She spun and danced, feeling like she was back in Enchantia, dancing with the bluebirds in the sky.

As she held the final position, her eyes glanced at Madame Za-Za and she saw her teacher nod and smile…

Two days later, Delphie raced up the steps into the ballet school. "Delphie!" her friend Lola said, running to meet her. "The cast list is up for the show!"

"Where?" Delphie gasped.

"It's outside Madame Za-Za's office!" Lola's eyes shone. "Oh, Delphie. I'm a robin, Poppy's a deer and you're the…"

Delphie didn't hear any more. She was already racing to the door at the end of the corridor. A piece of white paper was pinned up with the characters and

next to them the name of the person playing that character.

Delphie's eyes found the first line:

The Bluebird… Delphie Durand.

Delphie could hardly believe it.

"It's brilliant you're the Bluebird, Delphie!" Lola said, running up behind her.

"Look! Sukie's the rabbit!" Lola giggled. "She's *so* not going to be happy about that!"

Delphie didn't care what part Sukie had. All that mattered was that she had danced for joy in the audition and that she owned a pair of magic ballet shoes. She turned a pirouette in delight. *What could be better than that?*

*Tiptoe over the page to learn
a special dance step...*

Darcey's Magical Masterclass

Delphie's *Demi-Plié*

*Try one of Delphie's favourite ballet moves,
a demi-plié. It's one of the first steps
that ballet dancers learn...*

1.
Stand in first
position,
resting your
left arm on
your *barre*.
Make an oval
shape with
your right arm.

2.
Bend your
knees, keeping
your heels
together. Make
sure they don't
leave the
ground!

3.
Raise your right arm up in a soft curve.

4.
Now straighten your knees and lower your arm gently, until you are back in your original position.

(P.S. Not everyone has a *barre*, so you could rest your hand on a wall or fence instead.)

Magic Ballerina

Delphie and the Masked Ball

Delphie is really excited about the end of term ballet show. But while she is waiting in the wings, her help is needed in the magical world of Enchantia. Can she get there in time to save the masked ball?

Read on for a sneak preview of book three...

Delphie landed with a bump and looked about, expecting to find herself in the theatre again, but instead she was in a large round bedroom that had a four-poster bed and a white fluffy rug on the floor.

"Delphie!"

A beautiful girl with long brown hair came hurrying over from the doorway, her hands outstretched in greeting. "Princess Aurelia!" Delphie gasped.

"What's the matter?" Delphie asked the princess, "Is it King Rat again?"

"Yes. Oh, Delphie, look!" Aurelia pointed out of the window.

Delphie turned around. What she saw made her stare. The beautiful palace courtyard below was full of animals and birds – cats, dogs, horses, deer, goats and birds of all different colours.

"What's happening? Why are there so many animals in the palace?" Delphie asked in astonishment.

"They aren't animals," Aurelia said miserably. "They're my parents' friends! King Rat has changed them all – perhaps forever!"

°ⓞ˙*˙☆ ⓞ˙*˙☆ ⓞ˙*˙☆ ⓞ˙*˙°

Darcey Bussell

Buy more great Magic Ballerina books direct from HarperCollins
at **10%** off recommended retail price.
FREE postage and packing in the UK.

Delphie and the Magic Ballet Shoes	ISBN 978 000 728607 2
Delphie and the Magic Spell	ISBN 978 000 728608 9
Delphie and the Masked Ball	ISBN 978 000 728610 2
Delphie and the Glass Slippers	ISBN 978 000 728617 1
Delphie and the Fairy Godmother	ISBN 978 000 728611 9
Delphie and the Birthday Show	ISBN 978 000 728612 6

All priced at £3.99

To purchase by Visa/Mastercard/Switch simply call
08707871724 or fax on **08707871725**

To pay by cheque, send a copy of this form with a cheque made payable to
'HarperCollins Publishers' to: Mail Order Dept. (Ref: BOB4),
HarperCollins Publishers, Westerhill Road, Bishopbriggs, G64 2QT,
making sure to include your full name, postal address and phone number.

From time to time HarperCollins may wish to use your personal data
to send you details of other HarperCollins publications and offers.
If you wish to receive information on other HarperCollins publications
and offers please tick this box ☐